Other Lothrop, Lee & Shepard Books
by Jan Ormerod
Sunshine, Moonlight, Rhymes Around the Day,
101 Things to Do with a Baby, The Story of Chicken Licken

First U.S. Edition
1 2 3 4 5 6 7 8 9 10

Library of Congress Cataloging in Publication Data
Ormerod, Jan.   This little nose.
Summary: When Baby gets a nose cold, Mom cheers him up by showing
him the noses on a doll, cat, and teddy bear.
[1. Nose—Fiction. 2. Babies—Fiction. 3. Sick—Fiction] I. Title.
PZ7.O634Th 1987   [E]   87-2605
ISBN 0-688-07276-3

This Little Nose

Jan Ormerod

LOTHROP, LEE & SHEPARD BOOKS

NEW YORK

This little nose
is red and runny.

This little nose
is round and black.

This little nose
　　　is a very little nose.

This little nose
is a long nose.

Who's a poor,
little, grumpy person?

Who's a nosey,
furry fellow?

Two little noses
close together.

You'll feel better
in the morning.